ONE, TWO, THREE

STICKER AND DRAW

This edition published by Parragon Books Ltd in 2016 and distributed by

Parragon Inc.
440 Park Avenue South, 13th Floor
New York, NY 10016
www.parragon.com

Copyright © Parragon Books Ltd 2016

Written by Susan Fairbrother
Illustrated by Abigail Burch, Lauren Lowen, Ana Seixas, and Ruby Taylor
Consultant checked by Geraldine Taylor
Edited by Laura Baker
Designed by Karissa Santos and Clare Phillips
Production by Charlotte McKillop

ISBN 978-1-4748-2053-0

Printed in China

ONE, TWO, THREE

Note:
To get the best learning out of this book, it is recommended that an adult work alongside the child.

PaRragon

Bath • New York • Cologne • Melbourne • Delhi
Hong Kong • Shenzhen • Singapore

Look at all the balloons!
Touch each one as you count each bunch.

4

5

1.

Just 1 of everything.

1 volcano ...

1 tree ...

1 big dino
coming ...
run, run,
RUN!

1 sun ...

Sticker **1** ladybug,
1 dragonfly, **1** bush,
1 rock, and **1** puddle!

Find **1** of each of these.

nest

flower

sun

volcano

cloud

Here is **1** smiling cat.

2:

Your turn ...

Now there are
2 smiling cats!

Whose boots?
Ready, draw!

2 boots make a pair ...
2 perfect pairs of boots!

3 :

Let's loop the loop the loop! Trace and stick.

Whee! It's number 3!

The **3** billy goats gruff found a safe way across the bridge! Sticker the smart goats.

4

Color ...

Trace ...

BOp!

1

2

Beep!

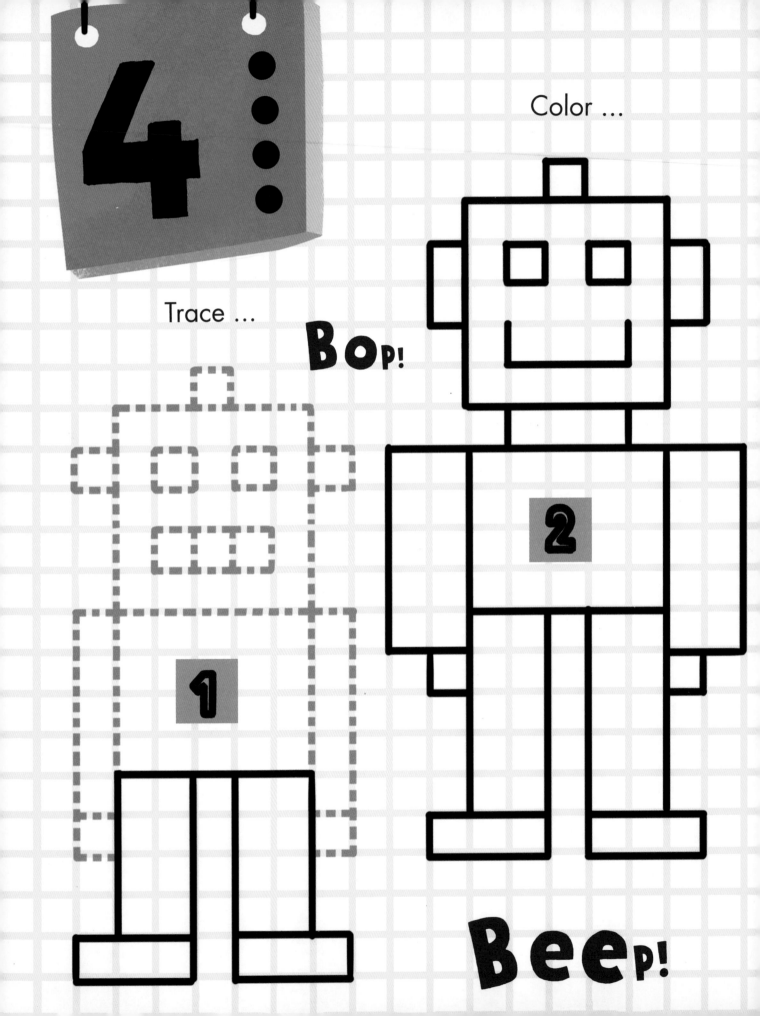

Stick ...

Doodle!

BOOp!

4

3

Blip!

5 ⦂⦂

Here's **1** cow.

Magic beans for sale!
Price: **1** cow for **5** beans

Now sticker Jack's **5** beans!

Stick **5** golden eggs in the nest.

Look at that beanstalk! Color it green.

Sticker a magic bean at the bottom.

Wow, more balloons!
Count the bunches.

9

10

tall

small!

Sticker the missing birds.

1

6

2

3

4

5

6!

Oink!

Roar!

7 ⠿

The nose knows!
Whose noses are those?
Draw a face around each one.

Trumpet!

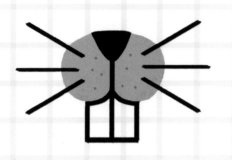

MUnch!

Ooh-ooh-aah-aah!

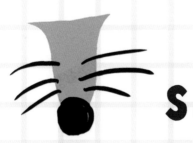

Squeak!

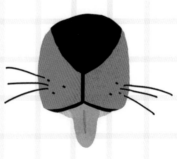

Woof!

8

Warm up chilly Octopus with **8** sticker mittens.

That's better!

10

Sticker the missing birds to make **5** groups of **10**!

That's really
impressive!

Color **5** red cars, **2** green cars, and **3** blue cars.

Ahoy there!

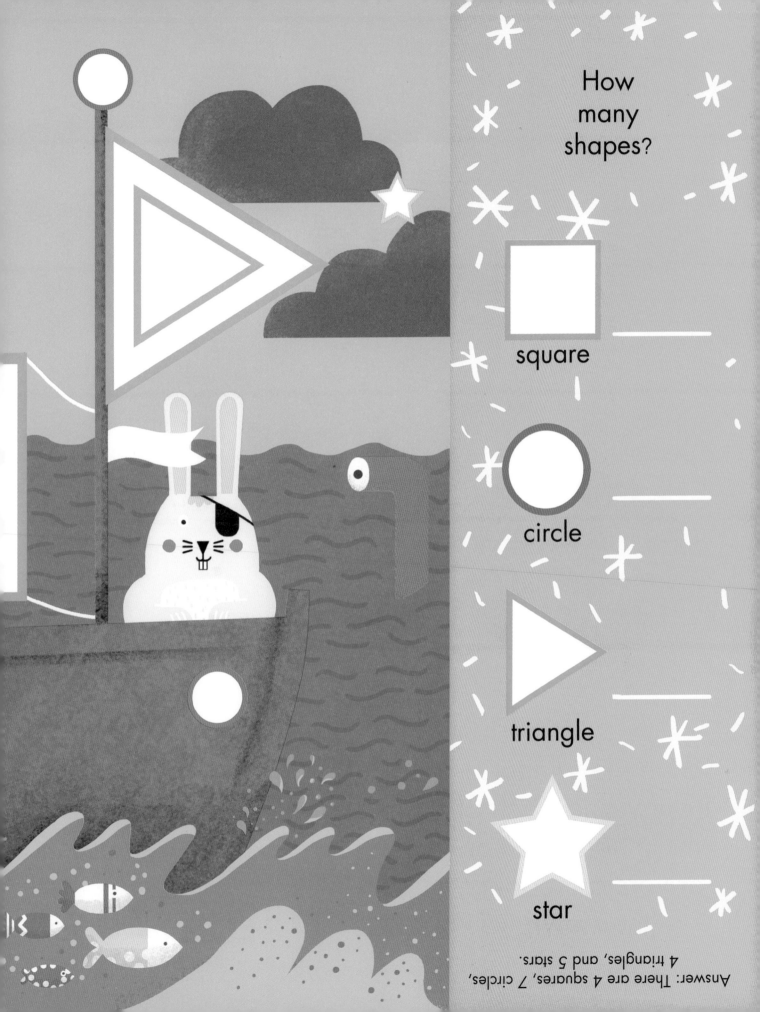

How
many
shapes?

square _____

circle _____

triangle _____

star _____

Answer: There are 4 squares, 7 circles, 4 triangles, and 5 stars.

3, 2, 1, go!

Give the winner a trophy and each of the other race car drivers a medal of their own.

1st

2nd

3rd

4th

5th

10 hungry hamsters!

Sticker **1** piece of food on each hamster's plate.

Have you ever seen such a magnificent palace?

20 of everything, everywhere!

How many do you count?

Add stickers to make **20** of each!

Knock, knock! Who's there?

Add stickers to show whose house is whose.

3

4

LIONS
KEEP
OUT!

Does your
house have
a number?
What is it?

5

Cheep, cheep.
Sticker all the baby birds!

0 zero

1 one

2 two

3 three

4 four

5 five

6 six

7 seven

8 eight

9 nine

10 ten

5 balloons up high

Pop all **10** with a matching **POP** sticker. Naughty kitten!

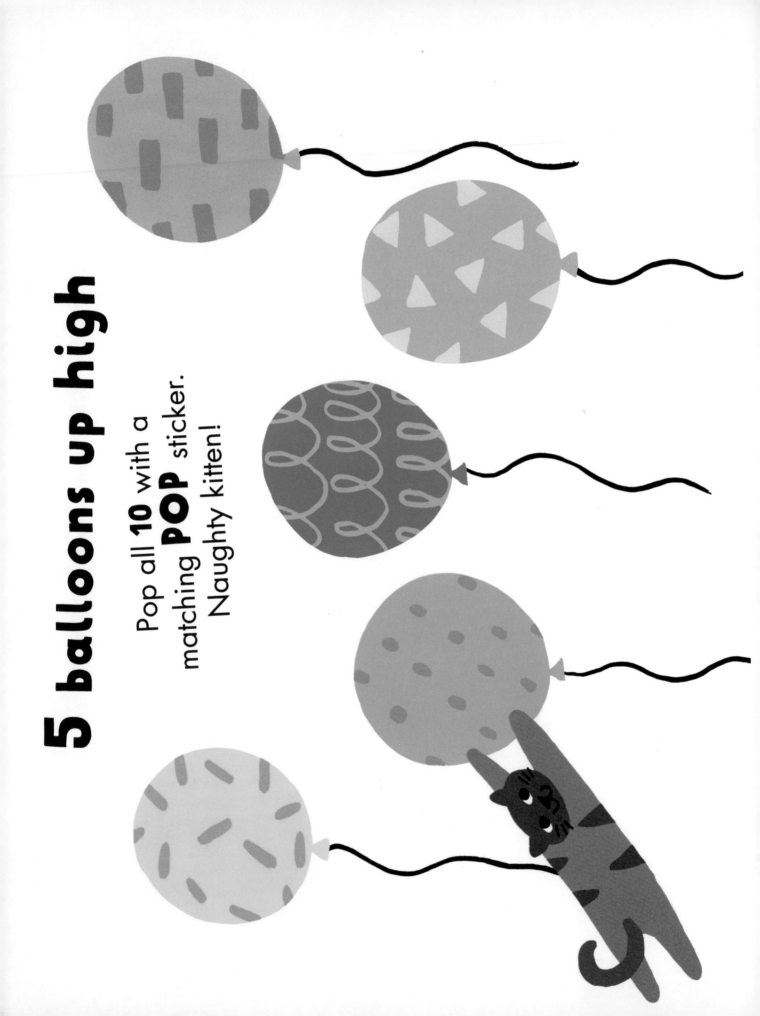

5 balloons down low

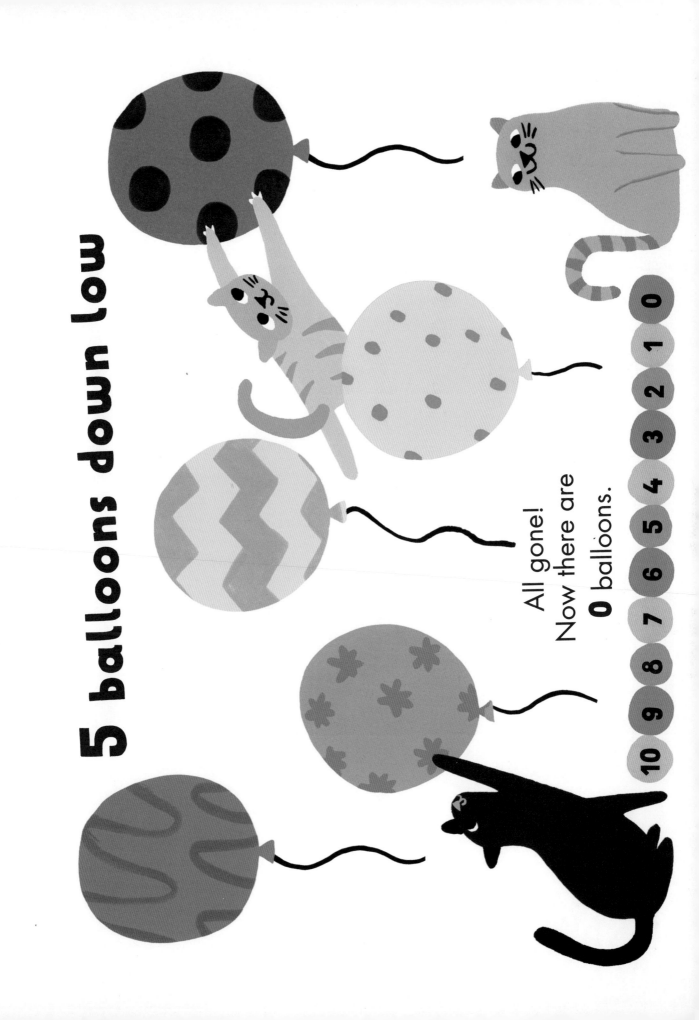

All gone!
Now there are
0 balloons.

10 9 8 7 6 5 4 3 2 1 0

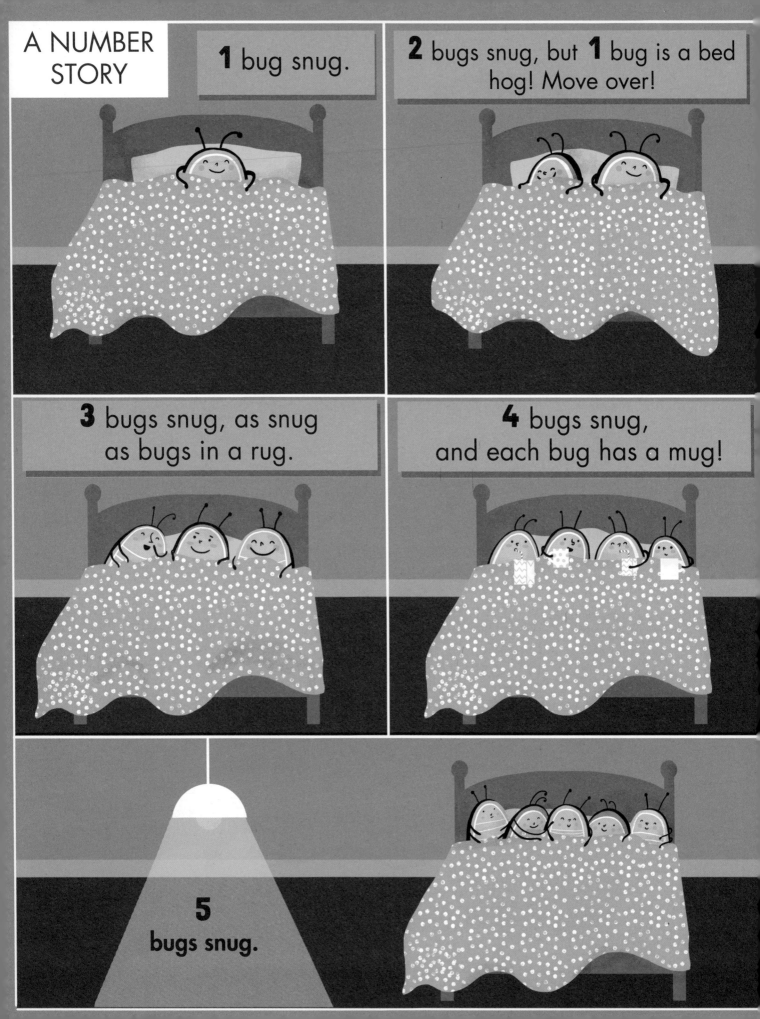

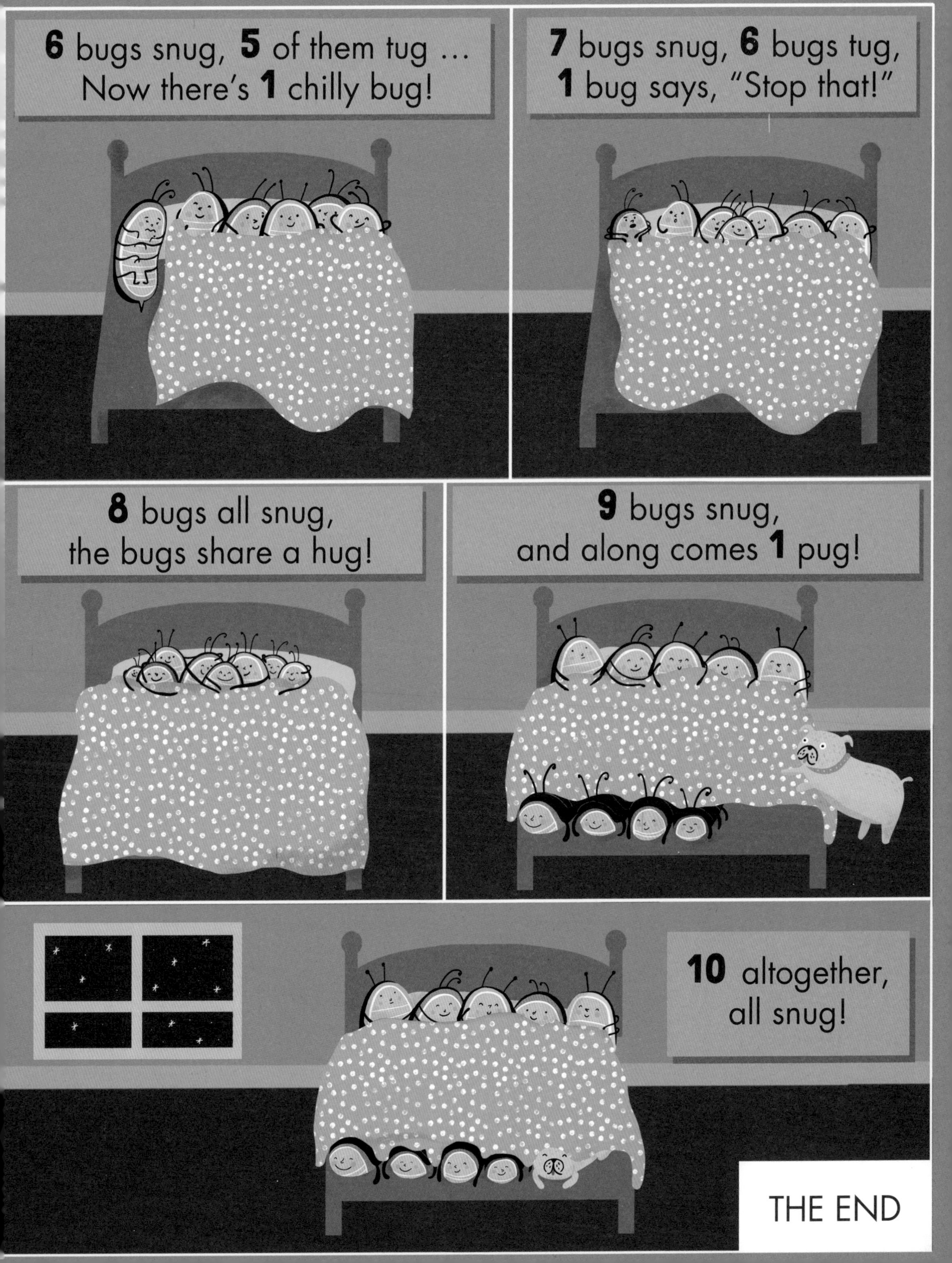
6 bugs snug, **5** of them tug …
Now there's **1** chilly bug!
7 bugs snug, **6** bugs tug,
1 bug says, "Stop that!"
8 bugs all snug,
the bugs share a hug!
9 bugs snug,
and along comes **1** pug!
10 altogether,
all snug!
THE END

Triple trouble!

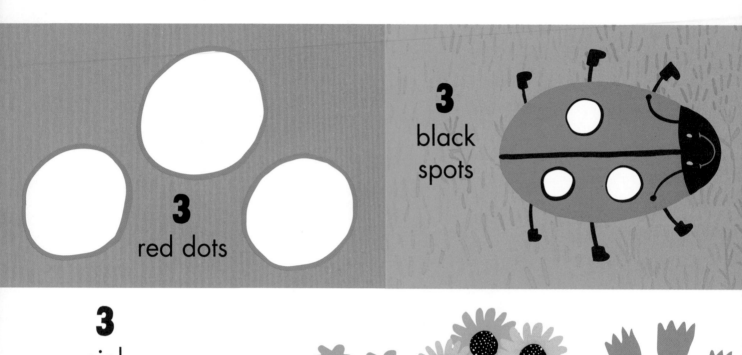

3 red dots

3 black spots

3 pink flowerpots

3 purple robots

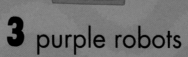

Way up
high!

Whee!

Sticker **5** little monkeys
jumping on the bed!

Way down
low.